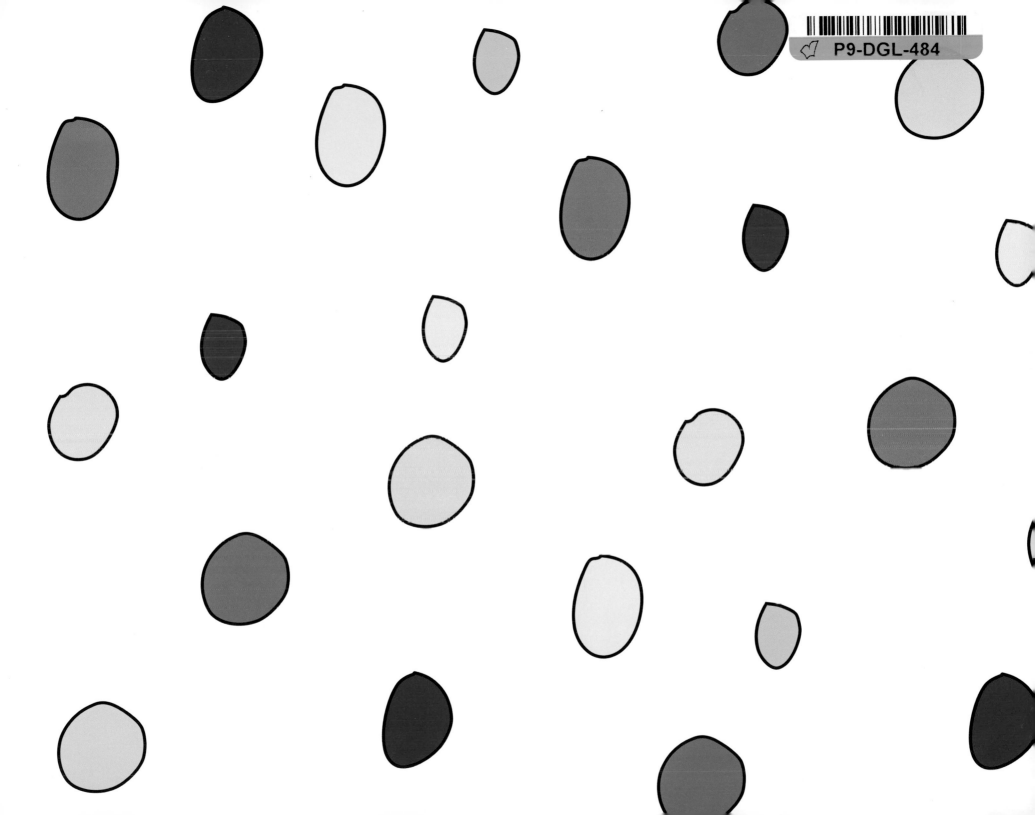

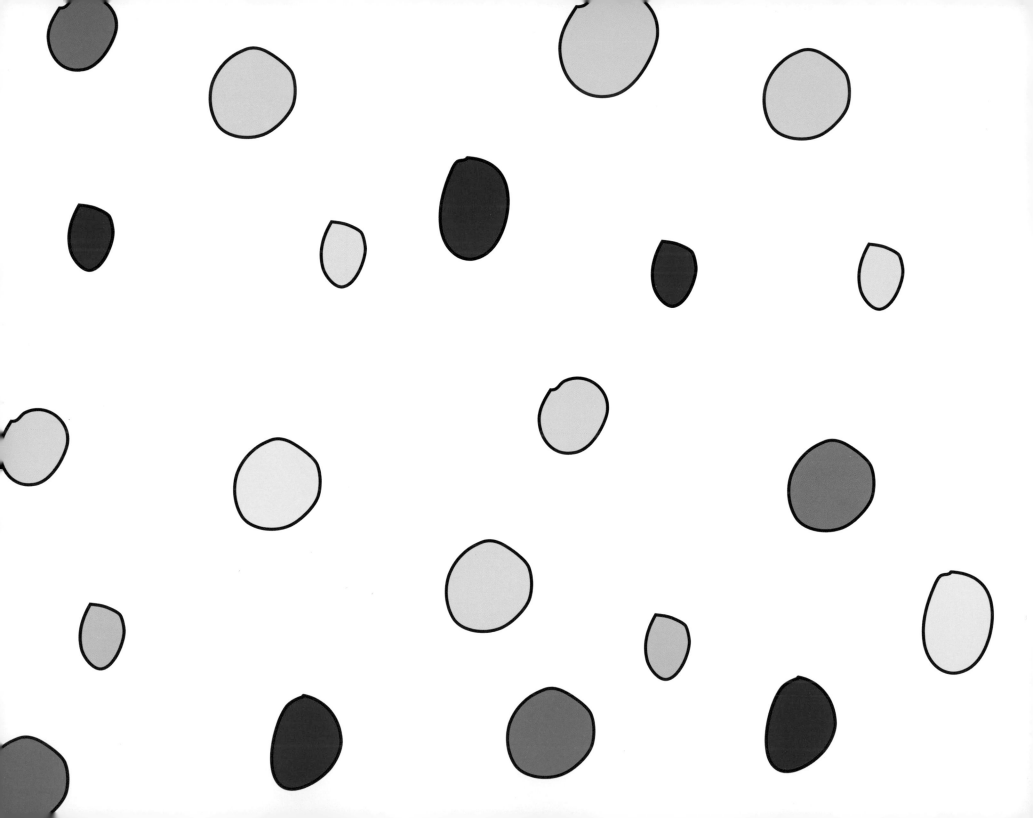

YOU!

by Sandra Magsamen

Life's a big
adventure
just waiting for you.
Give it all you've got,
there's nothing
you can't do!

Never stop **exploring,** 'cause life would be boring!

Be clever and curious, just like a cat. Ask lots of **questions** about this and that.

Look at life from **different** points of view. Turn things upside down if it suits you.

Wake up in the morning and holler "**Hip, hip hooray!**" Everyday is inviting you to smile, shine, and play!

Climb great, tall mountains and **reach** for the sky. You might fall down but then you will fly!

Remember, you can **be anything** you really want to be, like a pilot, a poet, or someone who lives in a tree.

Try not to say
words like,
"I can't, I won't
and I should."
Instead
think...

"I **can**,
I **will**,
I **did**, and
I'm **good!**"

Don't be afraid to make a mistake or two. It might lead you to **discover** something new.

Dream big

and remember to follow your heart. Believe in yourself 'cause you're really so smart.

When you grow up and do all that you do,the most important thing is just to **be...**

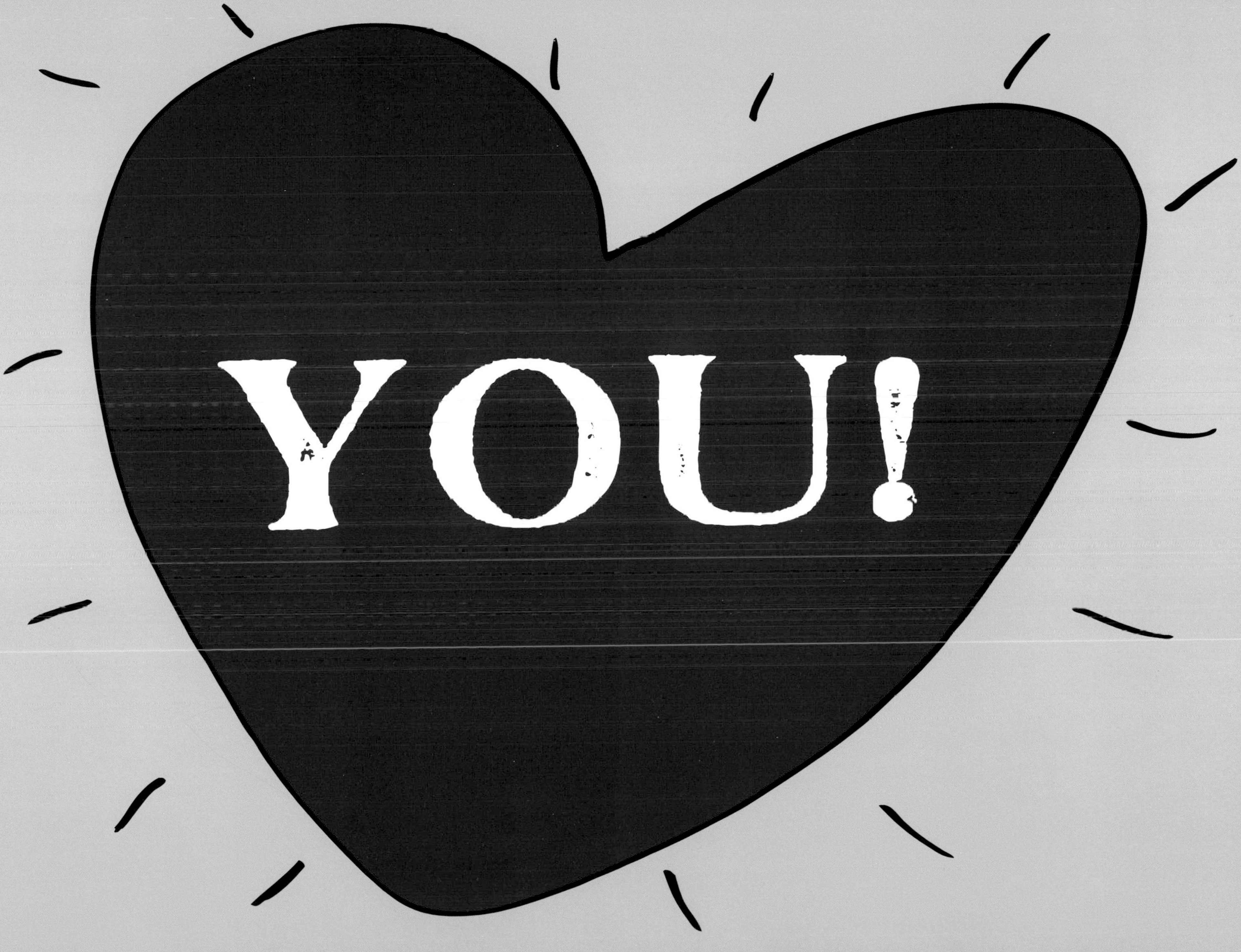
YOU!

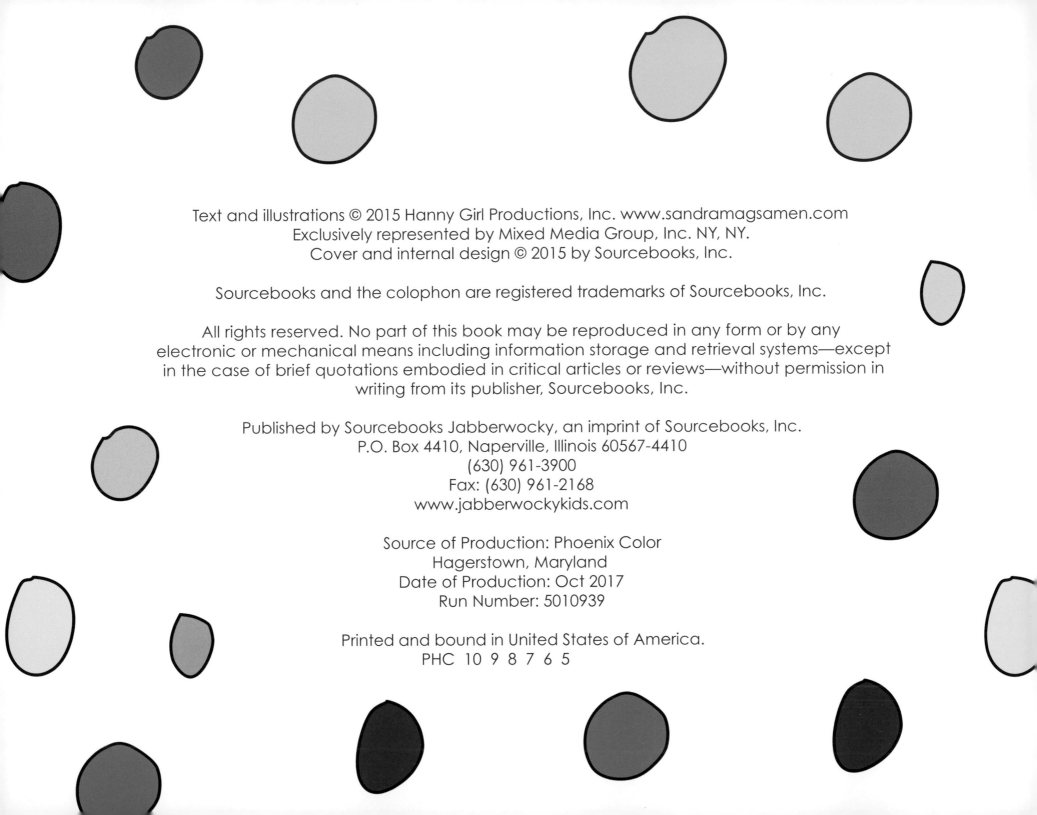

Published by Sourcebooks Jabberwocky, an imprint of Sourcebooks, Inc.
P.O. Box 4410, Naperville, Illinois 60567-4410
(630) 961-3900
Fax: (630) 961-2168
www.jabberwockykids.com

Source of Production: Phoenix Color
Hagerstown, Maryland
Date of Production: Oct 2017
Run Number: 5010939

Printed and bound in United States of America.
PHC 10 9 8 7 6 5

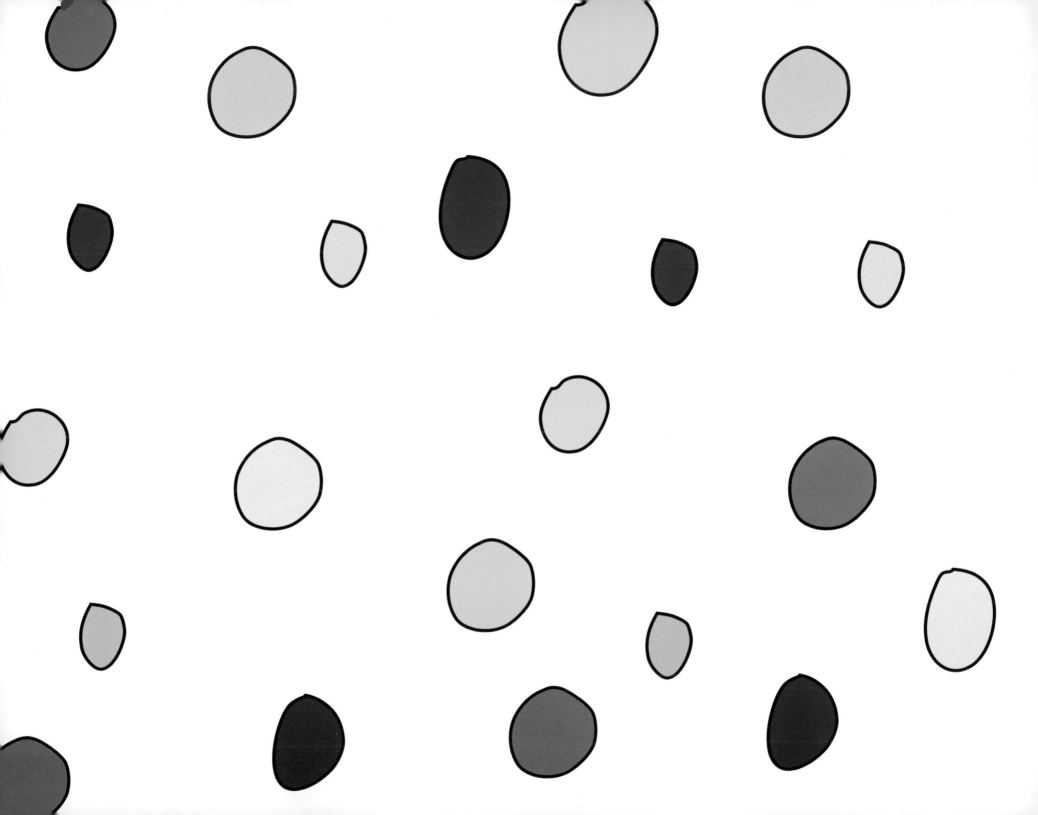